A story of accep[tance]

people for who they are and never losing sight of your dream...

Dedicated to...

My loving family "Team Barry"
who inspire me everyday

In memory of Frankie,
forever our best friend
2006 – 2019

KEEP THE TAP ON

Written by Paul Barry

Illustrated by Sarycheva Natalya

This is Terry, a normal seeming frog,

He lives in a pond and sleeps on a log.

Despite being green and just like his army,

Terry does something that drives all the frogs barmy...

Terry's a tap-dancer, he thinks it's so neat.
With tap-dancing shoes on his
tap-dancing feet.

A top hat and a cane clutched firmly in
hand, Terry's the greatest dancer in all of
the land.

The rest of the frogs look on in dismay, when Terry's been dancing the whole tip-tap day!

The army are always putting him down, "Here he goes again, acting the clown!" Terry's the happiest frog that you'll ever meet, tapping along to his tip-tap beat.

Terry will tap-dance whatever the season. From winter through spring, he needs no reason.

In wind, sun, rain and snow,
Terry keeps dancing in his tip-tap flow

They'd clap and they'd cheer, and they'd shout 'Encore!
And this inspires Terry to dance even more.

He dreams of becoming a West End star.
People would come from near and far...
to watch him dance up on the stage,
men, women, children, whatever their age.

Oh no, oh dear, Terry's woken up Dad!

He was fast asleep on the lily pad!

"Enough is enough!" Dad says with a hop,
"This dancing all day, must stop, stop
STOP!

Leave this pond now, no more I say,
we've all had enough, hop off, go away!"

Terry is banished and walks away in despair.
This doesn't seem right; it just isn't fair!?

The frogs look on with a sigh and a phew!
As Terry disappears from everyone's view.

Not a tip, not a tap, not even a peep, as
Daddy Frog stretches and goes straight
back to sleep!

The next few days, no sound could be heard.

A tap-dancing frog, how utterly absurd!
The army get on with their daily frog jobs,
Not hearing Terry's faint, gentle sobs.

Though sent away, Terry continues to dream, as he sails on a lily pad, heading downstream.

He won't give up, the army might scoff, but Terry's tap will NOT be turned off.

He WILL be a star; he WILL dance on stage.
Men, women, children, whatever their age.

Clapping, cheering and shouting 'Encore!'
He'll just keep tapping, more, more and
more.

Back at the pond and as time goes on,
it feels so different since Terry has gone.

If truth be told, it's got a bit boring.
The only sound comes from Daddy frog's
snoring!

The frogs think of Terry, the joker In the pack, They miss the fun times and want their friend back.

"Maybe Terry wasn't that bad!?
I know he drove us all a bit mad, but at
least he brought some fun to us all, maybe
Tap-dancing is pretty cool?"

"TERRY COME BACK!" they ribbit together.
"Bring back your dancing, today and forever!"

The army decide to shout out his name.
They feel truly sorry and completely to blame.

A movement in the bushes and out pops Terry!
He jumps over a log, ducks under a berry
The army look on with a smile on their face

Terry always brings joy to this place!

"Who are we to tell you to quit?"
It isn't your fault, not ONE little bit!"

"Follow your passion, dance with delight"
"Tip-tap all day and into the night!"

He hops back over and starts his tip-tap.

Terry grins as they all start to clap.

Learn to accept someone for who they are.
Everybody follows a different star.

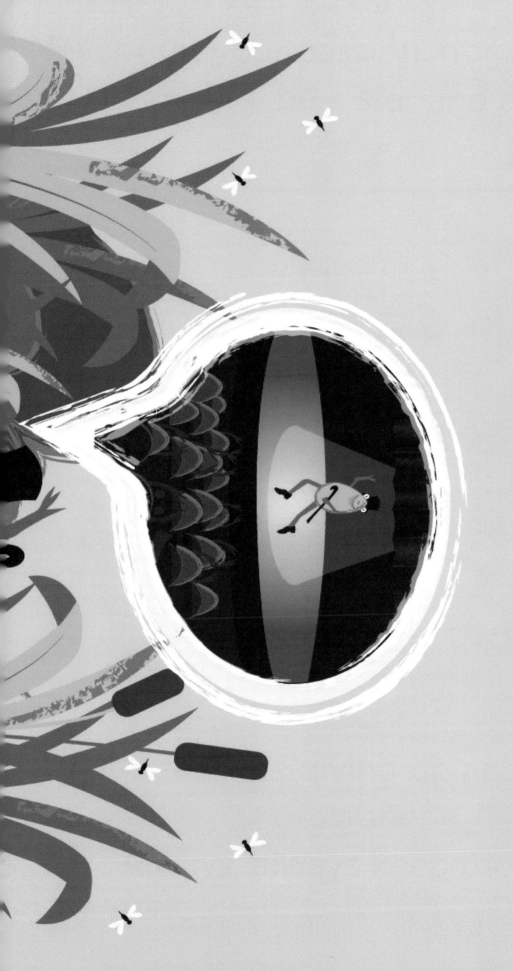

Everyone joins in with his bouncy grooves,
a hop and a skip, in their tip-tap moves.

Don't let people ever dash your dreams.
A dancing frog's not as daft as it seems!
Ignore all the doubters, let your light shine
through.
One day your dreams may really come
true.

Never quit your passion, not anytime soon,
Dream big, be a star and aim for the
moon.

If you feel like giving up and all hope is
gone,
Always, always keep the tap on.

<u>A few thank you's...</u>

To my wife Jo and daughters Lucia and Sophia for listening to my stories and always giving me honest feedback!

To Sarycheva for her hard work and commitment with the brilliant illustrations.

To Alex Lake for helping me to understand the importance of scanning and structure. Grown ups, check out his books, they're amazing!

And finally, to you for buying and reading this, my first book! I hope you and your family enjoy it for many years to come.

<u>About the author...</u>

Hi, I'm Paul and thanks for buying my book! I have always had a dream to write my own children's picture story and one day, be able to read it to my daughters. My real job is as an Academy Football coach working for a Premier League Football Club, but in my spare time, I like to write short, quirky little stories exploring some of the lessons in life that I've learnt in my time. I hope you've enjoyed reading about Terry and never lose sight of achieving your dream!

Printed in Great Britain
by Amazon